DYBBUK
A STORY MADE IN HEAVEN

By FRANCINE PROSE
Pictures by MARK PODWAL

 Greenwillow Books New York

For Bruno and Leon
—F. P.

For Bernie
—M. P.

AUTHOR'S NOTE

Though a dybbuk made its first literary appearance
in the seventeenth century, belief in dybbuks and other
troublesome spirits can be traced back to early Jewish
folklore. From 1912–1914, the Russian playwright
S. Ansky formed the Jewish Ethnographic Expedition
and traveled in Eastern Europe, collecting Jewish
folktales and legends, proverbs, songs, and recorded
music. He based his famous 1918 play, *The Dybbuk*,
on the material that he gathered, just as I based my
version, loosely, upon Ansky's.

Bibliography:
Ansky, S. *The Dybbuk and Other Writings.* New York:
Schocken Books, 1992.

Trachtenberg, Joshua. *Jewish Magic and Superstition:
A Study in Folk Religion.* New York: Atheneum, 1970.

Gouache and colored pencils were used for the full-color art.
The text type is Esprit Medium.
Text copyright © 1996 by Francine Prose.
Illustrations copyright © 1996 by Mark Podwal
Printed in Hong Kong by South China Printing Company (1988) Ltd.
First Edition 10 9 8 7 6 5 4 3 2 1

Library of Congress Cataloging-in-Publication Data
Prose, Francine, (date)
Dybbuk: a story made in heaven / by Francine Prose ;
pictures by Mark Podwal.
    p.   cm.
Summary: Forty days before a baby is born the angels in heaven
decide whom it will marry; therefore, nothing prevents the wedding
of Leah and Chonon from taking place.
ISBN 0-688-14307-5 (trade).   ISBN 0-688-14308-3 (lib. bdg.)
[1. Jews—Europe—Folklore.   2. Folklore—Europe.]
I. Podwal, Mark H., (date) ill.   II. Title.   PZ8.1.P9348Dy
1996   398.2'089924—dc20   [E]   95-22825   CIP   AC

Forty days before a baby is born, the angels in heaven
get together and decide whom the baby will marry—
when the baby grows up, of course. A boy from here,
a girl from there—the angels match up the happy
couples.
And so it was decided that Leah would marry Chonon.
But first they had to be born and grow up.

Leah grew up, pretty and smart,
in the little town of Chopski.

And Chonon, miles and miles away, became a brilliant
student with the kindest heart and the loudest sneeze—
Achoo!—in the little town of Klopski.

Eventually Chonon went to study with the Grand Rabbi of Chopski, where he moved into a rented room—in Leah's family's house.

When Leah and Chonon met, they fell in love at first sight. (Well, not *exactly* first sight—the angels had introduced them forty days before they were born.) Then Chonon got nervous and started to sneeze—*Achoo!*—so loud that storm clouds of feathers flew from the pillows and the family's best dishes wobbled dangerously on the shelf.

Leah and Chonon decided to marry, just as the angels had planned.

But because Chonon was a student and poor, Leah's parents had other plans. They wanted her to marry Mean Old Benya, the most powerful man in Chopski.

One day Leah told her mother that she and Chonon were in love.

That afternoon, when Leah went to the market, her father ordered Chonon out of the house—and out of Chopski.

"Besides," Leah's father told Chonon, "my daughter is planning to marry Old Benya."

In despair Chonon went back home to the little town of Klopski. And everybody could hear him sneezing sadly—*Achoo! Achoo! Achoo!*—miles and miles down the road.

That night Leah asked where Chonon was.

"He's gone home to Klopski," her mother said.

"To get married," said her father.

"Guess who's coming to dinner?" said her mother. "Mean Old—"

"*Nice* Old Benya," interrupted Leah's father.

Soon after, Leah—in despair—agreed to marry Old Benya.

Everyone began preparing for the marriage. It was to be
the grandest wedding ever celebrated in the little town
of Chopski. The fiddlers tuned up their violins, the
bakers baked a mountain of cake and bread, the cooks
borrowed every kettle in town and made an ocean of
chicken soup.

On the day of the wedding Leah's cousins and aunts came to help her get dressed.

"I don't want to," said Leah, in a deep low growl . . . and a trace of a Klopski accent.

Her aunts and cousins stepped back. "Why is her voice so strange?" they asked. "She doesn't sound like herself at all! And she looks so . . . faraway and peculiar!"

"A tiny sore throat," Leah's mother said. "No reason to be alarmed."

But as they approached the synagogue, Leah's voice got deeper. And as the women led her under the wedding canopy, Leah looked even more faraway, and she growled at Old Benya, "You are not my bridegroom!"

"That doesn't sound like Leah!" said the guests. "She sounds like a young man . . . with a Klopski accent!"

"Take her away!" shouted Old Benya, who wasn't called Mean Old Benya for nothing. "I don't intend to marry a girl who sounds like a man from Klopski!"

"She sounds like my student Chonon," said the Grand Rabbi of Chopski.

But no one heard, because Leah's parents were shouting, "What will happen to the mountain of cake and bread? To the ocean of chicken soup?"

"Eat it yourself!" growled Leah, in that deep, scratchy voice.

"Someone do something!" cried Leah's mother. "Bring her some chicken soup!"

"I don't want chicken soup!" snarled Leah. But she bent her head over the peppery soup and sneezed so loud— *Achoo! Achoo!*—that the fluffy wedding cake collapsed and the fiddlers dropped their fiddles.

"Now I know what has happened!" said the Grand Rabbi of Chopski. "Your beautiful daughter has been possessed by a dybbuk!"

"A dybbuk?" exclaimed Leah's parents.

"A dybbuk?" exclaimed the guests.

"Well," said the Grand Rabbi, "sometimes it happens that the angels pick someone for us to marry, forty days before we are born, but we ignore the angels' plans. . . ."

Then Leah shouted in that throaty voice, with that Klopski
accent, "I am Chonon! I am Chonon! I want to marry Leah!"
And she tore up the marriage contract.

Leah's mother fainted. As soon as she opened her eyes, she
asked, "What can we do? How can we cure her?"

"Well," said the Grand Rabbi, "sometimes it happens that
if a person marries the right person, the person the angels
pickcd out for them, the dybbuk leaves the person's body. . . ."

"Send someone to Klopski," Leah's mother said. "Send someone to get Chonon."

"Not so fast," said Leah's father. "If it is a dybbuk—and let's say it *is* a dybbuk—then we must call Rabbi Pinchik, who knows the magic spells for driving out dybbuks."

So Rabbi Pinchik was summoned and came with his anti-dybbuk equipment.

The villagers put on white prayer shawls and blew
very loud on black shofars. Then they lit black candles
and arranged them in a circle around Leah, and the
smoke rose toward her nose. . . .

"I command you, Dybbuk," said Rabbi Pinchik.

"Leave this young woman's body!"

"*Achoo!*" Leah sneezed. "*Achoo! Achoo!*" And all
the candles blew out.

"Let's try again," said Rabbi Pinchik, and he relit the candles.

But again Leah sneezed, and all the candles went out.

"I am Chonon!" said Leah in that gravelly voice. "And I want to marry Leah."

"You know," said Rabbi Pinchik, "I don't think this is working so well."

"Do something!" cried Leah's mother.

"I don't know . . . ," said Rabbi Pinchik.

"Excuse me," said the Grand Rabbi of Chopski. "As I was saying earlier . . . about the angels having chosen someone for your daughter to marry . . ."

"All right! I give up!" Leah's father said. "Send someone to Klopski. Send someone to get Chonon."

So a messenger raced to Klopski to invite Chonon to a wedding—his own!

And Chonon raced back to Chopski so fast that the soup was still bubbling in the kettles, and the fiddler's violins were still in perfect tune.

"Hello, Chonon!" said Leah, in her normal sweet voice. The faraway look disappeared from her eyes, and she smiled.

"Hello, Leah!" said Chonon, and he sneezed so loud— *Achoo!*—that it seemed like a signal . . . to start the wedding!

Never had such a fine wedding been celebrated in the town of Chopski. The ocean of soup was guzzled down, all the cake and bread were eaten, the fiddlers fiddled for three days and nights and did not run out of songs to play.

Even Mean Old Benya sang and danced, and from that day on everybody called him Nice Old Benya.

So Leah and Chonon were married and lived happily ever after, and they never again were possessed by dybbuks or spoke in anyone's voices but their own.

Chonon was appointed the Assistant Grand Rabbi of Chopski, and he and Leah went on to have many happy children for the angels to match up with husbands and wives . . . forty days before they were born.